ICARUS

a novella

L.E. Teetzel

ICARUS

ISBN: 978-1-0689433-1-7
second edition

this one is still for B.

I originally wrote this novella in 2017-2018 for a contest. Since then, it has sat on my website and in the files of my computer, waiting for me to figure out something to do with it. Or, rather, what I *wanted* to do with it.

In rereading it recently, I realized there's a lot more of my mental health struggles in this sci-fi tale than I realized when I wrote it. While I've never struggled with drinking, there were times in my life when my depression and anxiety felt like another person in my head directing my life. This story takes that idea to another level.

In addition to depression and mental health issues, *Icarus* also deals with suicidal ideation, self-destructive behaviour, hallucinations, parental neglect, suicide (in the past and in mention), and violence in a battle setting. There is talk of drinking, blood, gore, and death.

And please, if you are struggling or suspect someone you care about is struggling, please reach out for/offering help.

Speaking from personal experience, it really does help when you have someone to help carry you through those dark thoughts and feelings.

Parts of *Icarus* don't sound like me anymore, and other parts sound very much like me, which only serves to complicate my feelings about this story. It's part of a larger world in my head, and I'm wondering lately if that world is worth exploring further or not. But *Icarus* deserves to see the light of day because I do like this story and someone out there might like it too.

<3

1.

I'm ten. We are outside in the grass, the scent of flowers heavy on the breeze and the indigo sky cloudless above us. March has dug his remote-controlled dropship out and is supplying imaginary troops with reinforcements in their fight against the Scaleheads. I'm sitting on the opposite side of the yard in the shade, reading a novel on my tablet. Our father is inside, unpacking and cleaning, upbeat music leaking through the open window, and our mother is deeper in the colony, dealing with one crisis after another as the settlement is built up around us. Strange, long-necked birds are singing somewhere nearby, their voices eerily human.

It is peaceful, just like every day on Icarus has been. Four perfect days. Paradise, like my parents said it would be. Paradise, like the name of the colony. It hasn't even rained here yet, though I seem to be the only one who minds. I like the rain.

Maybe leaving Earth wasn't the worst thing that could have happened.

I inhale deep and exhale slow.

March sees something and takes off running, his toy abandoned in the grass like it's been shot down. He is beyond the boundary of the yard and about to disappear from view, pointing at the sky with his other hand, shouting something as he runs, though I can't make out the words. I yell at him to come back; we aren't supposed to leave the yard. Outside its colonies, Icarus is not a friendly place. I hear the radio crackle inside, my mother's frantic voice distorted by static, and then my father is running out of the house and past me, towards March, his face twisted by panic and fear. A towel dangles forgotten from one hand, his arms wet and soapy to the elbows.

A flash of light and heat, and March and Dad are gone. Incinerated.

I try to scream and I can't breathe.

I woke up tangled in sweaty sheets, gasping for air. Dying.

My heart pounded in my ears as I clawed at the loop of fabric wrapped around my neck, my lungs burning and my chest tight. I could still feel the dream, the *memory*, at the edges of my consciousness, still hear March's laughter leaking into reality as I fought for air. I squeezed my eyes shut when my vision started to go black and pulled with all the strength I could muster.

The sheet finally fell slack.

Air rushed into my lungs and I coughed, my stomach rolling and bile creeping up my throat, sour and hot and tinged with the taste of the cheap wine from the night before; it tasted vile going down and even worse coming back up. I coughed some more, opened my eyes—they roamed wildly, taking in my surroundings: bare white walls, black sheets, bluish light leaking through the gaps in the curtains illuminating the clothes and bottles and books strewn across the floor.

My apartment on Earth, not the prefab structure on Icarus.

Twenty-five. Not ten.

I remained still for a moment, my chest rising and falling as I forced myself to take slow, deep breaths, and the world came back into focus. My brother continued to laugh, mocking instead of joyful.

Three times that week I'd had the dream—it was so much easier not to think of it as a memory—and three times that week, I had woken up dying, with that sound in my ears.

I never saw the truth version of that day when I relived it.

I hadn't been all that interested in what my younger brother was doing. I hadn't yelled at March to stop running. I hadn't told him to come back; let the favourite child get in trouble for once, I'd thought—I was going to stay where I was supposed to.

If I had called him back, March and Dad would probably still be alive, Mom probably wouldn't have killed herself, and I—

If you'd been a good big sister, Knox, you wouldn't be alone.

I sat up slowly and stared at March where he stood, visible in an exposed bit of window. Fear prickled along the back of my neck, the same way it did whenever I saw him. He wasn't laughing now, just glaring. It was the same expression I'd seen on his face when he first appeared to me in the window of Mom's hospital room after the doctors told me she was dead. It was the same expression he usually wore now, the innocence and radiance of childhood gone.

I was never alone; March was always nearby and I'd long ago accepted that I'd lost my mind.

He sneered when I opened my mouth to try and say *I'm sorry*, but the words never left my throat. As I met his eyes, the only thing that reached my lips was the desire for more booze to quiet the vision, the memory. The desire for oblivion.

Imagined heat washed over my face and I closed my eyes again, the adrenaline, grief, and guilt coursing through me and resolving into a headache throbbing at my temples and behind my eyes. My stomach cramped painfully as vomit burned a path up my esophagus.

March remained silent as I pushed myself off the bed and stumbled to the bathroom, his eyes hot on my back. I stepped on a broken wine bottle—shattered against the wall at some point, though I didn't remember throwing it and had only vague memories of cutting my hands to match the dried blood on the carpet—but the pain was distant, secondary to the images still etched in my head and the spasms in my gut. I threw up, got most of it in the toilet, and then pulled myself to my feet, leaning heavily on the vanity and slapping the wall with one hand until I hit the light switch. Under the harsh white light, I rinsed my mouth and splashed water on my face, hoping it would banish everything that wasn't real. No such luck. His face was there to greet me when I looked in the mirror, his features superimposed over my own.

You could have kept us alive.

I scowled. I wanted a drink to get rid of March and ease the pain for a while, but I'd drained the last of what I had the night before and made sure there were no more bottles stashed around the apartment. If I was drunk, they wouldn't let me on the shuttle, and I'd been waiting for years to be called up to serve on a long mission, for the chance to return to Icarus, and I wasn't going to screw it up now that it was here.

Besides, there were other forms of oblivion out there.

One of them being the cryogenic sleep waiting for me on the *ISC Altair*. I'd be frozen for nearly half a year, unconscious and out of March's reach. *You don't dream in cryo*—words from training I clung to.

Just let go, Knox. You don't have to be alone.

I took another measured breath and touched the mirror, bringing the digital display to life on the surface of the glass. Sixteen degrees Celsius, cloudy. 3:45 am. I'd slept for four hours and I had three hours before I had to be at the ISC base to catch my shuttle to the *Altair*. There was no way I was getting back to sleep, not with March around, and there wasn't time for me to run myself into a coma—another of my go-tos for getting rid of March and the memory.

I shook my head, then turned on the shower. Doing my best to ignore my intangible companion, I stepped into the too-hot water and scrubbed myself clean, scrubbed until I was pink all over, and then I just stood there, letting the water cascade over my head, obscuring my hearing and sight. I closed my eyes when March appeared in the shine of the tile to my left. Tried to pretend I was a regular person, one without the ghost of their little brother haunting the fried synapses of their brain.

But his voice was still clear, and my fantasy was no barrier.

Just let go.

I inhaled a mouthful of water with my next breath.

A wad of water, spit, and bile splattered against the floor of the shower as I coughed, and I had to catch myself against the wall to keep from slipping on the wet tile. March was laughing again, louder than before, almost maniacal. I felt tears in my eyes as I expelled the last of the water I'd inhaled, tears that began to fall as I righted myself and scrambled from the shower, turning off the water as I went. I dropped onto the bathmat and held my head in my hands, gasping wetly. A small trickle of watery blood spread from my sliced foot across the floor. Drool hung from my lips.

"Leave me alone," I choked out.

You don't want me to go.

Naked and dripping, I turned off the lights and left the bathroom, shutting the door behind me to hide the mirror. The only mirror in my bedroom was broken—another casualty of my dangerously active nights—so I made for the window, heedless of the bloody smears I was leaving on the carpet.

I intended to pull the curtains closed over March's transparent visage, but the familiar blue-gold lights of the *ISC Altair* flickering in the sky caught my attention, even through the fog and pollution clinging shroud-like to the city. I traced a line from the orbiting ship to the military base I could just see at the edge of the skyscrapers and apartment buildings making up the skyline, and imagined I could see the shuttle waiting for me and twenty-four other soldiers.

I'd joined the International Space Corps the day I turned eighteen, searching for something to hold on to after my mother's suicide and years in the foster system, and had never expected to see active combat; from all reports, we were winning, reclaiming the space the Scaleheads had taken and protecting our colonies.

Apparently, we weren't doing as well as the media led the world to believe. I'd been on four short missions in seven years, and I was just a member of the reserves, only called up when there was need for more bodies, though even then they usually only took those who volunteered. Like me.

I sighed and ran my fingers back through my wet, tangled hair before snapping the curtains closed and heading for the closet, where the only things hanging up were my uniforms.

Five hours until shuttle launch, ten until the *Altair* left Earth's orbit and I was frozen. In solitude.

Five months, fifteen hours until I was back on Icarus.

2.

The air outside was hot and thick, the temperature having skyrocketed with the first hint of sunlight, and it didn't take long for my last clean uniform to become soaked with sweat. I wanted to peel it off and go back inside to the air-conditioned cool, but the vision of March was still lingering and it would take more than heat and humidity to force me back to that. I had precious few minutes without his face haunting me. Of course, he could follow me outside—

My eyes flicked to the storefront window on my left, but there was no sign of my brother. Just my own pale reflection, eyes too dull and surrounded by sallow bruises.

I sighed, but the relief was short-lived, halted when I heard voices nearby.

I could feel the eyes of passersby tracking my uniform and

the purple reservist badges on my shoulders. Rationally, I knew they were wondering one of the countless things civilians did when they saw someone in uniform—Where is she going? How long will she be gone? Does she have any family she's leaving behind? I could never imagine fighting in space. I wonder if she's ever seen a Scalehead up close—but I couldn't stop the voice in my head, the one that had nothing to do with seeing my dead brother, from telling me they were looking at the bags under my eyes, the faint marks on my neck from my near asphyxiation, the slight limp in my walk as I avoided putting too much weight on my injured foot, and I was sure they could smell the booze leaking from my pores. I hunched as I walked and tried to blend into the sparse crowd.

They see you for what you are.

A shiver went down my spine, but I managed not to jump. I had grown too used to March's comings and goings to be startled by them. Too used to the patterns of my thoughts that usually summoned him. "Shut up," I muttered. I closed my eyes, fighting the urge to look at the nearest reflective surface.

Let go.

I kept my gaze forward as I reached the main gate of the International Space Corps Toronto base and wove my way through the chain-link fence maze to the enclosed booth and the bored guard inside. He was leaning against the wall with his arms crossed, but his eyes were tracking all movement outside. Nothing would get by him. March's face was just visible in the scratched Plexiglas of the booth, but I forced myself to look only at the guard. To act like nothing was amiss. I was pretty good at it by now.

"ID."

I stuck my wrist under the scanner, the chip under my skin briefly flashing blue as the computer read the information. The guard's head turned to one side, his eyes moving across the screen to his right as he scratched his stubbled cheek. A holographic keyboard appeared beneath his fingers and he typed something in before giving me a single nod and pressing the button to unlock and open the inner gate. It squealed a bit as the gears kicked into motion. I waited for it to open all the way and then headed into the base, a few butterflies stirring to life in my stomach.

I hadn't expected to be nervous.

I'd been waiting so long for a chance to go back to Icarus.

Maybe I was just excited.

I pressed one hand into my stomach as I walked, following the marked path to the launch pads on the far side of the base. The urge to flee home, to numb myself with a bottle of wine and the TV turned up too loud or to run until my legs wouldn't hold me up anymore was stronger now, and I thought I could hear March giggling. The urges weren't unfamiliar ones, ones I never felt I had any control over; I hated them. The headache that had never fully gone away began to pound again.

"You don't dream in cryo sleep," I muttered. The words were like a mantra, the promise of true solitude for the first time in years too alluring to ignore. A new kind of oblivion.

You can't hide, Knox.

"You part of wave seventeen?"

The voice was loud, close. I started, too lost in my inner drama to notice anyone approaching, and looked to my right and up at the big soldier who'd spoken. He looked friendly. Like he liked to chat. Trying not to frown, I said, "Uh, yeah."

"Me too. Launch pad Alpha-051, right?"

It didn't sound entirely like a question. I raised one eyebrow. "Are you really asking, or are you just making conversation?" My voice sounded rougher, lower than normal. A reminder I'd spent the morning throwing up and crying after somehow nearly choking myself to death.

My apparent companion didn't seem to notice, but I'd never seen him before, so that wasn't surprising. It wasn't like he had a reference to compare my voice to. He just grinned at me; yeah, definitely a chatter.

"You caught me. Talking always helps the nerves."

I looked him over as we continued through the base, heading for the shuttles I could now see parked in their designated spaces next to the lake. He was very tall, at least six-foot-four, had the muscled body of someone who worked out most days, and the attitude of someone who had spent considerable time on a military base, but he was a reservist like me—though his purple badges, and his uniform, looked much more worn than mine.

"*You're* nervous?" I asked.

"The whole idea of being frozen for months on end has always freaked me out a bit."

"Then why do you do it?"

He shrugged, the shoulder closest to me rolling. "Got

nothing left down here, like most of us," he said, briefly touching a small array of medals over his heart; I hadn't noticed them before. I only recognized a few of them—Battle of Eden, Battle of Charon, Battle of Kuiper—but there were maybe a dozen on his chest. "Why do you do it?"

I opened my mouth to say something along the lines of *same as you*, but I snapped my jaw closed before the words could come. That would open too many doors. Might make March come back when he'd been gone since I'd entered the base. And I had no desire to get to know the soldier better. Oblivion was easier to find when no one cared how you spent your time. Besides, we'd arrived in front of our designated shuttle and, though I was finding it hard to take those last few steps, it was as good of an excuse as any to shut up. The butterflies inside were fluttering madly and a cold sweat had broken out on the back of my neck.

You can't do this.

"Hey, you okay?"

The big soldier's hand appeared on my arm, the sudden contact jolting me back to the present. I flinched but didn't pull away. "I… Yes. Yeah, I'm okay."

He grunted his disbelief.

Annoyed at him and at myself, I climbed inside the shuttle and moved to a seat in the far corner, my palms sweating as I buckled myself in, and then, after saluting, I gave my name and rank to the officer on board when he made his way to me. He typed my name into his tablet, nodded, and turned to the next soldier in line. My head began to pound in time with my heart, my stomach clenching around the fluttering. I squeezed my eyes shut to try and block everything out.

"You sure you're okay?" my shadow asked as he settled into the seat beside me.

He doesn't really care.

No one cares.

He continued speaking when I didn't answer. "You don't look okay. This your first mission?"

"No," I ground out, opening my eyes. March winked at me from the dull shine of the patterned steel floor beneath me, then vanished. Was the voice in my head his? Or my own? "First long mission, though." My voice came out steadier than I would have expected given the riot inside.

Last long mission.

The big soldier smiled and I wondered how he could be so calm, especially when he'd already admitted to cryogenics making him uneasy. Now that we weren't moving, I could get a better look at him—anything to keep my mind occupied. He looked young, maybe only a few years older than me, but there were scars visible on his neck and hands and face speaking to a longer life, a steely glint in his eyes only the long-term fighters got. But if he'd been frozen on more than one occasion, that could be why he didn't look very old. Maybe he'd been born long before I had, seen more than I had, but spent more time in the ice, slowing his progression.

"What made you volunteer for this mission?" he asked, rephrasing his earlier question.

"How do you know I volunteered?"

"Because you might look nervous, but not like you're going to shit your pants, and you don't look resigned."

"Resigned?" I sure felt resigned to the choices I'd made. To my questionable state of mind and mental health.

The soldier pointed across the shuttle to where a group of purple-badged young people sat, still and silent, staring at the floor as the seats around them filled and the craft prepared for launch. They did look resigned. And scared. They looked like my reflection did every morning. But they probably looked like that because they were leaving loved ones and a life worth having behind, and there was a very real chance they wouldn't come back. Not because they felt stretched too thin between their past and their present, or because they were used to being haunted by their demons. They probably had no demons. There hadn't been that much time between the call for volunteers and the conscription order, so I doubted they'd had much time to process what was happening before they'd had no choice but to say goodbye.

"I… I lost my brother and father in the attack on Icarus fifteen years ago," I said quietly and before I'd fully processed the decision to speak.

The soldier beside me was silent for a short while. Long enough for me to start wondering why I was sharing details. He didn't care.

Most soldiers had stories like mine; it was nothing special. A lot of soldiers had even joined the ISC because of their tragedies, to seek revenge or vengeance, though they didn't always make the best soldiers or last terribly long. But humanity had been at war with the reptilian aliens for so long, it didn't matter why people wanted to join anymore. The ISC would take anyone willing and able into its ranks or its reserves, and when there weren't enough soldiers on active duty, enough volunteers, enough reservists to be called up, they would conscript. More meat for the grinder. There'd been two conscription orders that I could remember, and I'd volunteered before the last one as well, but that had only been a short mission to the Kuiper Belt, no cryo required.

"You ever hear the stories about ghosts haunting old machines? Like televisions or computers?" the soldier finally asked, just before the silence threatened to break me.

"What does that have to do with anything?"

He gave me another one-shouldered shrug. "Just something I think about whenever I'm getting ready to launch."

I frowned at the change in subject, but went with it. The less I had to share about my family, the better. Something told me the soldier had picked up on my reluctance. "And thinking about old ghost stories helps you? Our lives are going to be dependent on machines for the next five months."

He snorted. "My older brother used to tell me those stories during power outages, or when we were camping—anywhere it was excessively dark. I'm pretty sure it was his private mission to scare the hell out of me as much as possible, and those stories did it. Huh. Maybe those stories are the reason cryo freaks me out."

"You don't say." I felt one corner of my mouth twitch. "I've heard a few of those stories. Never gave them much credence though." A lie. But I wasn't about to tell the stranger I frequently saw my deceased brother in reflective surfaces. I wasn't going to tell him that I believed in ghosts.

"Go on a couple of these long missions, and you might change your tune."

I mentally revised my assessment of his age—he was definitely much older than me. I couldn't stop myself from asking, "Why are you just a reservist?"

He chewed on his bottom lip, like he was debating answering, but he hadn't hid any personal details thus far, and he didn't strike me as cagey. "Got bumped down a few years ago, after a Scalehead took my leg off and they had to build me a new one." He reached down to rap his knuckles against his right thigh and I heard a muffled metallic tune. "They offered me the chance to retire, but I said I'd just switch to the reserves while I was going through therapy, and they weren't about to refuse. Never got back to a hundred percent, so in the reserves I stayed."

Listening to him was making me calmer, and I realized it had been a long time since I'd had a conversation with someone that didn't include orders or buying something; I felt a pang of sadness at the thought that Emmy, the employee who always worked nights at the liquor store near my apartment, probably knew me better than anyone else.

It's your fault you're alone.

Come home to us.

"That's... I can't imagine spending my whole life fighting."

You're a liar.

"What do you do when you're not headed to space…?"

"Knox."

"Hi, Knox. I'm Dean. Nice to meet you."

An unexpected laugh bubbled out of my mouth at his cheeky tone. "Hi, Dean."

"So?"

"I work in a bookstore." A tiny, out of the way bookstore where, most days, I spent a great deal of time alone, attempting to lose myself in a book and ignore the thirst for booze and oblivion and dreamless sleep. A place where I could dream about going back to Icarus and getting rid of my ghosts as I stocked shelves and cleaned.

I won't be that easy to get rid of.

I caught a glimpse of March in the reflective panel across from me. His eyes narrowed and his lip rose in a snarl. I looked down at the floor, but he was there too.

"Huh. Never would have pegged you for a reader."

I was only able to give a weak shrug in response, March's reappearance having drained the levity of my conversation with Dean.

Dean must have taken my silence for nerves at the impending launch, because he gave me another grin just as the shuttle began to vibrate beneath us. The engines roared to life and the shuttle rose with a lurch, my stomach rolling, my heart beating hard in my chest—hard enough that my vision wavered and my breath caught in my throat. I closed my eyes and dropped my head back against the headrest, mumbling my mantra again under my breath, and concentrating on breathing evenly.

The vibration grew more intense as we climbed higher and, just before the secondary engine kicked in to push us into orbit where the *Altair* waited, my entire body went cold. I was light-headed. Dizzy. My headache ramped up to agonizing and I wanted to be anywhere but on that shuttle. I heard Dean calling to me from what sounded like a long distance away, and then I felt his elbow bump mine a second before my vision went black.

Let go.

3.

I am floating in inky darkness, still buckled into my seat, but the shuttle is no longer surrounding me. Dean and the other soldiers are gone too. I can move my arms and legs, and I don't appear to be moving forward or drifting sideways, though without something to mark distance, it's hard to be sure. There are no smells or sounds. I try and speak, but no noise comes from my mouth, and when I try to undo the buckles holding me in place, the latches won't unlock, no matter how hard or how many times I press the buttons.

I'm trapped.

I feel cold sweat soaking the back of my uniform and sliding down my spine, more and more until I'm drenched. My heart beats faster and faster and I pull at the belts with the same ferocity I used to free myself from my twisted sheets that morning. My fingernails scrape against the thick material. I think I can feel them pulling away from my skin. The belts tighten until they're digging into my flesh through the fabric of my uniform.

I stop. I have to stop.

Or I'll pull myself apart.

I scream and the lack of sound makes everything worse.

I am crying and thrashing, beyond all reason, when March appears.

He materializes from nothing and the abruptness startles me into stillness. He's floating through the darkness towards me, that nasty smirk on his face. It's not an expression he ever wore in life, but I'd long ago stopped expecting this spectre to act the same as the little brother I remember, the little brother I loved. My brother comes to a stop in front of me, floating high enough that he can look down at me and still reach my face when he extends his hand. His fingers are like ice.

"Why are you doing this, Knox?" he asks, his voice solid and real, unlike when he appears to me in the waking world. "Why are you going back? There's nothing for you there."

I try to answer, but still no words come out. I can feel tears sliding down my cheeks. My shoulder twitches as I attempt to reach out to March, but my limbs will no longer move. I am immobilized and, as soon as the realization crosses my mind, the panic sets back in. But I try not to let it show because I don't want to give March the satisfaction.

"Oh, Knox. You need to let go of all of this if you truly want to find peace."

March vanishes as suddenly as he appeared.

I scream.

This time, a piercing sound comes out. His definition of peace scares the shit out of me.

I came to, still on the shuttle, still buckled into my seat, still surrounded by soldiers, but with the world blurry and noisy and chaotic. Dean was sitting sideways in his chair, concern on his face and his buckles undone so he could lean towards me, getting in close to check my vitals; his fingers were warm on my throat. His lips were moving—I thought he was saying my name, but I couldn't seem to hear properly—and the creases on his brow deepened. I got the sense he'd been calling my name for a while.

Finally, his deep voice broke through the fog.

"Knox? Are you okay?"

"I… What… Did I pass out?"

"I think so. Soon after we took off."

I hit the release button on my chest and the belts fell away—thank fuck—leaving me free to inhale as deep as I could. Some residual panic from the dream released and I sagged forward, bracing myself with my elbows on my knees. I'd never passed out on a shuttle before. I hadn't even passed out during the high g-force training.

I wasn't the only one to have passed out though, if the

chatter around me was to be believed. I was thankful. At least I wouldn't stand out.

The breather was short-lived however, as the shuttle door opened and our wave of soldiers was ushered onto the *ISC Altair*, the massive cryogenic transport ship we would be taking to Icarus. Dean waited beside me as I rose, there to catch me if I fell over or passed out again, and then he and I fell in behind a group of the nervous conscripted. His presence was unexpectedly comforting.

You are weak.

March's eyes followed me through the corridor, bouncing from reflective panel to porthole, over and over as we walked. I couldn't enjoy the stars; I could feel his glare, but I could also feel Dean's eyes on the back of my neck.

Let go.

I kept my eyes forward, watching the sway of the braid of the woman in front of me, and concentrated on taking in the ship around me without looking at March. The corridor we were in was narrow, barely wide enough for some of the bigger soldiers to get through without hitting the walls, the portholes showed the starry expanse of space and the curve of Earth below us, and the metal panels making up the floor, walls, and ceiling were mismatched and patchy looking. The *Altair* was a long-serving ship and the mission we were about to embark on would be its twenty-fifth. If I remembered the reading I'd done on the ship correctly, it was the last ship in service that still used the original cryogenic system, and it was capable of holding up to twenty-five waves of twenty-five soldiers; we were wave seventeen, so there would be eight more boarding behind us. To me, there was something beautiful about the whole organized process.

Something about the visible control, I was sure. Control I sorely lacked.

We were led first into a locker room where we exchanged our ISC uniforms for skin-tight black thermal suits that would plug into the cryo-pods, and then into a massive circular chamber filled with three concentric circles of people-sized pods made of silver metal and black plastic, one central control station, and endless coils of different coloured wires. An ambient purple-blue light tinted everything, and coloured lights winked out from the various machines, sparking curiosity in me. I'd read a bit about the systems the ISC used to freeze its soldiers and colonists, but most of what I'd read had been lost in the oblivion I kept fighting my way back to.

I had been curious once, eager for knowledge rather than nothingness. Maybe I'd get back to that one day, but I doubted it.

Three white-coat-clad cryo-techs stood in the centre of the room, watching us file in. We all saluted the officer who'd guided us from shuttle to ship, and then he left, no doubt to head back down to retrieve another wave. I felt sweat bead up on my neck and along my spine. My palms began to itch and I rubbed them against my legs as subtly as I could, though the slick material of the thermal suit did nothing to dry my hands. So instead, I ran them back over my hair, smoothing wayward strands against the braid holding most of my hair in place, and tucking some behind my ears. The butterflies were back, churning my guts into a buzzing mess.

I wanted to go home. I wanted to get in that chamber. I wanted to run. I wanted to cry. I wanted to scream.

My solitude was so close, Icarus so far.

You don't dream in cryo.

March's voice in my head was mocking, and I did my best not to react. I stared at the pod closest to me hungrily, craving what it offered and thankful it wasn't reflective. Peace. Freedom from March, from what he represented, and from the memory-dream my subscience insisted on making me relive. I balled my hands into fists at my sides to keep from reaching out and crawling in before I was told. For the first time in a long time, I wasn't thinking of wine or running or numbness, I was thinking only of lying down, of being as good as dead for a while. Ceasing to exist without actually ceasing to exist.

Beside me, Dean exhaled through his nose loudly. I tore myself out of my head and looked at the big man. His hands were fists like mine, and his shoulders were creeping up towards his ears. He was chewing on the corner of his lip.

"Hey," I said quietly, nudging his arm with my elbow. "Cryo's the easy part." I was trying to joke, but the tone felt foreign, clunky on my lips.

Dean gave me a weak chuckle but, before he could respond, one of the techs stepped forward, touched his arm to get his attention, and led him towards his cryo-pod. I stood and watched, impressed that he could go through being frozen when he was so visibly unsettled, when I knew he was afraid. I didn't need to see him on the battlefield to know Dean was brave. Selfless.

Something in my chest clenched. I would never be brave or selfless; the only reason I was going to the front line was to deal with my own demons, to make my life easier—

Or end it.

My chest spasmed again, like a hand was tightening around my heart and lungs, and my vision wavered briefly—

I'd never had that thought before. I didn't want to die.

Did I?

What was going on? Being in space had never made me react so intensely before, and I'd been looking forward to cryo for so long. Certainly, nerves weren't the cause of this.

"Private First Class Abernathy?"

The technician who approached was younger than me. Cryogenic freezing may have made it difficult to determine age, since things like smooth skin and shiny hair were no longer sure signs of someone's years, but I was pretty sure the tech hadn't spent too much time on ice. He was too bouncy, too excited. His eyes were too bright.

Or maybe I was just jaded.

"Yes."

"Perfect." He checked something off on the small tablet affixed to his arm with a stylus, and then slapped his hand against the transparent plastic lid of the pod in front of me. "Step on up and we'll get you ready for your nap."

I closed the distance between me and the pod and peered into the open space: a thick pad where I would lay, a series of needles and tubes that would connect to the suit, and a few belts to hold me in place should the ship's movements be anything less than smooth. When the lid was closed, I would only be visible from the waist up, since most of the pod was made out of opaque material. I swallowed and pressed my fist to my stomach, kneading in a vain attempt to pacify the fluttering.

"Are you ready?" the tech asked.

I gave him the most indignant look I could while standing there in the skin-tight thermal suit. The temperature of the chamber around us was dropping steadily, but the fine trembling working its way along my limbs was due to more than just the cold. "If I said no?"

The whip-thin tech pressed his lips together to try and stop his laugh. He ended up snorting. "Point taken," he said. "All right then." He tapped the side of the pod with the metal stylus he'd been spinning in the fingers of one hand. He was always in motion. "Hop in."

I swung my leg over the edge and shimmied into place, my emotions continuing to bounce between excitement and nervousness. I was counting on the solitude, but it was hard to stop thinking about my earlier conversation with Dean—my life was going to be directly connected to this machine for the next five and a half months, and while the technology was well-tested, things still went wrong. People still died while they were on ice. About half the last batch of reinforcements hadn't even made it to Icarus because of a malfunction that cut the power to all their pods, and then cut the emergency backup power as well. That was why the technicians and crew would all be awake and warm during the journey, to keep an eye on everything and everyone and do all they could to prevent a catastrophic failure. To get our boots on the ground, to fight the Scaleheads.

Although, as I watched my tech fidget his way through his final checks, I couldn't say that knowledge instilled much confidence.

I inhaled a deep breath, let it out slow, and looked around for any sign that any of the others were experiencing the same mix of fear and exhilaration as I was. Someone to my left threw up, and somewhere else in the massive chamber, another soldier was praying, their fingers clicking over a rosary. Someone else was bouncing up and down, smacking their chest to psych themselves up; they gave a wild whoop before nearly leaping into the pod. Dean, the only familiar face, was already in his pod—the one next to mine—eyes closed and breathing deep, and he wasn't the only one. You could tell who among our group had been frozen before and who was going under for the first time.

The tech, whose name tag read "Dr. Z. Kasagi," watched me make my survey, and offered a crooked smile when I met his gaze.

"There's no going back now," I muttered.

You don't dream in cryo.

The tech snorted another laugh as he set about hooking my suit into the pod. I felt my body begin to cool almost immediately as the cold saline moved through the miniscule tubes in the suit. There were several pinches in my arms and legs as the cryo-solution was injected. My eyelids started to get heavy, my thoughts slow. I heard music, the song Dad had been listening to on that day, echoing around the chamber in a dreamy cadence. Or just echoing around my head.

"What's the Z stand for?" I asked as the tech fastened the belts around my torso and hips.

"Zebadiah, but you can call me Zed."

"M'kay. Don't let me die, Zed." I blinked, and it was a chore to open my eyes again. "I don't wanna let go. Not yet."

"No need to worry, PFC Abernathy."

"Knox."

He smiled at me. His face wavered, like I was looking up at him from under water. "I'll make sure you make it to Icarus, Knox. Just keep breathing for as long as you can," the tech told me from what seemed like very far away. "The sedative will put you to sleep soon and…"

I never got to hear the end of that sentence.

The sedative knocked me out; the last thing I thought of before sleep took over was how, when I was little, the sedative the medics tried to use when I broke my arm made me violently sick. My brother had told me scary stories as I lay in bed, ones about ghosts haunting houses and haunting people, and ones about astronauts and soldiers going mad in space.

He had thought it would make me feel better.

I just wanted to make you smile.

March's laugh chased me into oblivion.

4.

I am ten again, sitting on the grass outside the prefab house in Paradise colony, my tablet clutched in my hands. I can feel the prickly grass against my legs, the smooth metal of the tablet in my hands, the breeze on my cheek. I can smell the sweet air, hear the creepy birds calling to one another. Everything is tangible. Real. But unlike previous mental journeys back in time, I am aware of what's happening, and I know this is a dream.

But it's a dream I shouldn't be having.

You don't dream in cryo.

I had spent hours in civilian and military training sessions, first as a settler, then as a soldier, listening to experts telling us that being frozen meant you were essentially dead to the world, telling us we wouldn't dream, and we wouldn't remember anything of our time on ice. We would wake up months later, in another part of the galaxy, and continue on like no time had passed. You might get sick. You might feel disoriented. But that was all after you woke up.

You don't dream in cryo.

So why am I here?

I put my tablet down in the grass and stare at the individual emerald blades for a few seconds, listening to the music coming from the house and to my dad's off-key singing. Had he been singing that day? I remembered him singing at other times— Christmas, New Year's, birthdays—always loudly and off-key, but I don't remember his voice before the chaos. I look across the yard to where March is playing. He's yelling something across the road to his friend, who's outside in her front yard; I think her name is Riley, but I'm not sure. They met as soon as we arrived at our new home, Riley having moved in the day before, and became friends in the immediate way young kids did. Had Riley been there that day? I don't remember seeing anyone outside my family.

I narrow my eyes, confused. This isn't how I usually see this day.

A loud noise splits the air—a ship entering the atmosphere—and everything stops. The colony goes silent around us, and March, Riley, and I all crane our necks to look up at the sinister grey-green ship slicing through the air towards us, towards Paradise, trailing smoke and clouds. It is no effort for me to imagine the red-orange eyes of the Scaleheads inside, shining as they prepare to destroy Paradise and all the humans who call the colony home.

I am not afraid. I am resigned to what comes next—what always comes next.

An alarm starts shrieking, shattering the silence and kicking everyone into gear.

Dad runs out the front door, screaming at March and I to get inside, but March is already gone, taking off down the street, his curiosity and craving for adventure getting the better of him. I know I can't stop what's about to happen, so when Dad looks over his shoulder at me for a brief second and tells me to get in the house, to get safe—Did he do that back then?—I nod, and, fighting the urge to let the fire engulf me too, I head inside, shut the door, and put my back against it. I know it won't make a difference to reality if I die in the dream, so there is no point in letting it happen. I wrap my arms tightly around myself and slide down to the floor, curling into the smallest ball I can.

Heat erupts through the windows.

The air becomes thick with the smell of burned plants and metal and flesh. A sharper smell I know to be burning scales mingles with the others and I fight to suppress a gag.

I close my eyes and cry.

I will never be able to save them.

You didn't even try.

When I open my eyes, I am still in the house on Icarus, though the sun is shining through the windows, and everything smells and sounds normal. I stand up using the door as support and spin in a slow circle, taking in the building around me. It's been a long time since I've thought about the inside of the house. I never see it when I dream. It smells a little like new plastic, and I don't remember it being this pristine. It's mostly pale grey, with bits of white and black and chrome, and everything is utilitarian in design. Luxury and frill will come later, when Paradise is settled and safe.

"Knox, you've got to come and see these flowers!"

March's voice, distant, a memory, pulling me from my rumination. Words from our first day on the planet. This is not March, the personification of my madness, my guilt.

"Come on, sweets—you can't stay inside forever."

Dad.

My heart lurches.

Faint singing is one thing, but it's been ages since I heard my dad's voice, and I know it's not distorted by time and my mind, because the deep timbre resonates in my chest and tears fill my eyes immediately. Hearing his voice is like coming home and I can't bear it because I know I'll never hear it again in the real world, never put my head on his chest when I hug him, never smell the particular mix of orange soap and vehicle grease and metal that took root in his skin after years of manual labour. A wave of emotion crests through me, pulling a soft sob from my lips.

Tears slipping down my cheeks, I open the front door and stand on the front step where I can see March and Dad sitting in the grass, surrounded by a patch of amethyst flowers, playing some made-up game. Dad laughs and my tears fall faster; I thought I had forgotten the sound.

When March lifts his face however, and his eyes meet mine, any happiness I was finding in the moment evaporates, and dread drips down my back like sweat, pooling in my stomach, turning everything sour. His face splits in a grin, morphing from cherubic child to sinister spectre in an instant. Dad looks at me with hate in his eyes.

I open my mouth to speak, to apologize, to beg for forgiveness, but no words come out. The air around me grows hotter and hotter under their gazes, until I feel the tears on my cheeks evaporate, the inside of my nose dry out, my lips chap. In the distance I can see great waves of fire approaching, moving faster than fire should have been able to. I want to run but I am rooted to the ground. The fire leaks between the buildings across the street and still March and Dad stare at me, one smiling, one accusing.

The fire takes the shape of a Scalehead army, figures eight feet tall stalking towards us, thick tails swishing violently behind them, setting the grass ablaze. They walk right through my family and neither March nor Dad make a sound as they turn black and die, the scent of their burning flesh making me wish I had more tears to shed, but I am dry as a bone.

One of the Scaleheads reaches me, their clawed hands extending to grab my arm. My parched skin begins to burn before they touch me.

I close my eyes and promise myself I won't scream.

I hope to find myself somewhere else when I open my eyes, but there is a sinking feeling in my gut that proves prophetic. I am still in Paradise, but it is Paradise as I have never seen it before.

Everything is on fire.

I'm inhaling smoke and ash and my heart is racing. I'm on my knees in the grass, twisted and charred human and Scalehead bodies littering the ground around me, the smell of burnt meat and scales filling the air, far more potent than anything I've smelled so far in this twisted journey, and maybe even in reality. I am dehydrated and I'm exhausted and I can hear sobs and gasps tearing their way through my nose and throat—at least I am not silent this time, at least I am not on fire.

But I am still helpless.

March appears before me without pretense, nothing but the sneering spectre I'm used to seeing. His form is more solid here, his gaze heavier, and he is definitely not human, not my little brother. I want to tell myself he's not real, like I did when he first appeared to me in my mother's hospital room, but that's never gotten rid of him before, so why would it work here, in this dream I shouldn't be having and can't control? Here I am at March's mercy. I am seeing what he wants me to, experiencing what he wants me to.

And he's as angry as ever.

Unlike before going on ice, when I just let things play out, I return March's glare—the best I can while I'm choking on every breath. I am still afraid, but I'm tired of this. I am tired of having my solitude stolen, of seeing my dead brother in every reflection. I'm tired of having pleasant memories dangled in front of me and then torn away. I am tired of reliving this day and feeling my brain unravel a lobe at a time.

I struggle to my feet and my breaths turn to rough, hacking coughs. My mouth fills with blood, the copper tang momentarily drowning out the other smells and the taste of ash on my tongue, but I force myself to keep staring March down.

"Stop—this," I manage to say, though it's a far cry from the order I meant to issue.

"I'm just trying to give you what you want, Knox. You've been fighting for years. It's time to let go."

He takes a few steps towards me, gliding more than walking. I stumble back before I can stop myself, something grabs my ankle, and I fall, landing hard on my ass, the shock riding my spine all the way to the top and dazing me briefly. March appears an inch away from my face, his body phased through my legs, a spot of cold in the inferno of Paradise. I look down and there is a hand clutching my ankle, flakes of charred skin hanging from pink bones. It's wearing Dad's wedding band.

"This is all for you, Knox. I am doing this for you. Let go."

I try to speak and the words are lost to the coughs racking my body. March begins to laugh when it becomes clear I can't breathe. His fingertips sink into my cheeks, a parody of a tender caress. Cold spreads through my body, travelling along my veins and through muscle and bone until I am paralyzed once again, until I can't think. He steals whatever air is left in my lungs.

"I—don't—want—to."

Every word is a challenge, a knife in the flesh of my throat. I narrow my eyes as March slides his hands all the way into my cheeks and reaches back until his fingers touch my spine. Around us, the fires rage, devouring every remnant of Paradise. All that's left is heat and the scent of burning and March's eyes boring into mine, his being reaching into my core, disrupting what it is that is me.

The moment my heart stops, I feel it, like a fist slamming into my chest.

"It's time for you to let go, sister."

I shatter, breaking into a million shards of ice that evaporate in the heat.

I wake to thunder, rumbling overhead. For a moment, I can't figure out where I am, other than I'm somewhere outside. It takes far too long from my brain to catch up and remind me that I'm not outside, I'm in space, frozen in a pod watched over by Zed, and then everything comes back in a rush, and I let out a shallow cry, roll onto my side, and curl into a ball.

I will myself to wake up, for the ship to reach Icarus, for something, anything that will bring relief from this steady torment. All I wanted was the solitude of cryo and the chance to face my demons head on, back where it all began. I didn't want this.

Of course you didn't want this.

March's voice startles me into stillness. When I'm sure all I can hear is my blood pounding in my ears, I slowly uncurl and stretch out on my back, staring up at the dark clouds above me, listening to the thunder, waiting for March to show up, waiting for Dad to make his appearance. Maybe even waiting for Mom, though she didn't die on *this* day.

But nothing happens.

I don't let myself relax. I'm not in control of these dreams, these nightmares.

I sit up and look around. I'm in the front yard of the house on Icarus, near the tree I was reading under before the Scaleheads came. But I'm alone. No March, no Dad. No… Paradise.

The house and I are on an island, surrounded by choppy black water, no other buildings or people in sight.

I stand up and walk towards the edge of dry land, scanning the horizon for any sign of life, or even for any sign of my ghostly brother. There is nothing. When I reach the edge, I look down. The water laps hungrily at the edge, little caps of white foam building against the rock and grass, and for a few seconds I watch the depths for…

I'm not sure what.

I'm about to turn away, try the other side of the island, when I see something pale beneath the water. My brow furrows as I watch it rise, and I prepare myself for the worst, tensing until every muscle is coiled. The thunder is loud above me.

The pale shape turns into a face and I go cold.

It's Dad.

Beside him, Mom rises from the deep.

Both are paler than in life, their lips are tinted blue, and their eyes are foggy and unseeing. I'm kneeling before I can think too much about what I'm doing, reaching out to them. I don't know what I intend to do. Pull them out? Hold them? Say goodbye? Dad's skin is clammy and he's too soft beneath my fingertips and I withdraw my touch before they sink into his rotting flesh.

Bile turns in my stomach. I clench my jaw shut and sit back on my heels, watching my parents float just beneath the surface of the dark water.

Above me, the clouds finally open up, and the rain is refreshing, soothing, even though it soaks me to the bone in only a few seconds. I continue to stare down at the water, almost wishing March would appear, because at least his anger is something I understand, something I am used to dealing with. I am not used to this.

The rain picks up and I lean forward until my forehead touches the grass.

Hands appear on my shoulders, the touch comforting at first, and it takes vital seconds for me to realize what's happening. As soon as I do, the fingers curl into the fabric of my shirt and haul me into the water, plunging me under and holding me there. Unable to get a deep breath in my shock, my lungs are straining much sooner than they would be if I'd been prepared, and then I am gasping down water, unable to handle not breathing any longer.

Let go, sister.

"We couldn't save her."

The words are indistinct at first, spoken through water, and when I finally realize what's being said—where I am—my world collapses around me. I feel weak, faded, and all I want to do is lie down. Sleep. I don't want to revisit this. I don't want to see it twisted by March's malice—it is already twisted enough.

I am wet, dripping on the tile floor, but instead of floating in some abyss, I am standing in the sterile hallway of a hospital. The hospital where the ambulance brought my mother and me after I found her lying in a pool of blood in the bathtub and called 911. In front of me stands a doctor, tall and strong, like Dad had been. He is wearing all white, and the computer on his left wrist is transparent except for the screen and the blue outlining the keys. On it, I can see a flat line that, minutes ago, had been pulsing with my mother's heartbeat. He is watching me with concerned eyes, but I don't have the strength to look up at him.

She was all that I had left and now she's gone. Faded out of existence. I wasn't enough for her to hold on for. I wasn't enough for her to survive for. Mom hadn't wanted to live in a world without Dad, without March—couldn't bear it any longer than the three years she'd ghosted through.

But she had been okay leaving me to a world without her.

Without any of them.

I fall to the floor, legs incapable of holding me up anymore, and I am ice cold.

I think I feel rain, but it's only me crying.

The doctor picks me up. At thirteen, I'm not small, but he holds me, carries me, like I weigh nothing at all, and rubs my back with firm and soothing strokes, and I let myself put my head on his shoulder and imagine he's my dad.

For the first time in my life, I voluntarily imagine I am back in Paradise—

And then I am.

I'm standing in the grass outside our house, staring at the lawn where March should be playing. He is not there. In fact, the whole colony is quiet around me. The world is quiet. There are no birds singing with human voices, no people talking, no children laughing, not even a breeze rustling the leaves of the nearby trees. My dad is not in the kitchen washing the dust from unpacked dishes. My mom isn't working somewhere deeper in the colony, putting out metaphorical fires to make Paradise a better place to live.

I am alone.

I walk across the yard to stand beneath the lone tree; one of the only trees within the colony that was here before us, that somehow managed to avoid being cut down when the first soldiers and engineers made space for people to live here. Most of the other trees are skinny and small, planted after all the prefab structures were put in place to make the place feel more homey, more like Earth. The bark is rough beneath my palm. I rub my hand against it.

"A hell of your own making."

I am unsurprised by March; I felt him coming, heralded by a cold breeze. At this point, I don't think I can be surprised by him anymore.

"I asked you to come with me in the hospital."

"I remember," I whisper.

In the centre of the yard, a transparent hospital bed appears and a younger version of me is lying upon it, the wavering form of March sitting at my feet, where he'd appeared after first showing up in the window. His expression is pleading. I can hear his words.

Mommy's here with me and Daddy now. Everyone's dead, 'cept for you. Let all of it go, Knox, and you could be here with us. You could be happy.

I had denied him then, sure he just some manifestation of my grief, and every time he appeared after, he was angrier, meaner. All that was left of my brother evaporated until he became the cruel, snarling ghost before me. The one bent on torturing me, on leading me to death one way or another.

"You are alone."

"I am alone."

"You have nothing."

"I have nothing."

"Let go."

I open my mouth, about to say the words, but force it closed. I don't want to let go. I don't want to die. I…

I don't know what I want, but I know I want to live.

And I know I want March, whatever he is, gone.

The air around March grows colder and spreads out, curling around me in a familiar way. Outside the vortex of cold, the air turns blistering. There are tears on my face; it hurts. I close my eyes, breathe deeply, and tell myself I can't die here. This is a dream.

You don't dream in cryo.

Dreams can't hurt you.

March screams, a high-pitched wail that drills right to my brain and makes my eyeballs ache. It gets colder, colder, colder—harder to breathe, impossible to see…

I am dying.

I am dead.

5.

I came to with the sterile smell of the hospital clinging to the inside of my nose, and the taste of freezing air on my tongue. I was cold. Heavy. Scared and confused. My chest hurt, like a pair of giant hands had wrapped around my ribs and squeezed to just before the point of breaking and then let go, and there was a bone-deep pain in my arms. I couldn't make sense of what I was seeing or feeling. Everything was blurry and indistinct, tinted purple-blue, and far too close to me. I couldn't move.

I was still in the pod, strapped in.

Why was I awake? I shouldn't be awake.

I'd died, hadn't I? In the dream, I'd died.

Was I alive?

Was this the next stage of my subconscious torture? Was this March's doing?

A red light flashed to my right, outside the pod. Sparks, I thought.

My pod was malfunctioning.

Panic smoldered in my gut. All other thoughts were replaced with the need to escape. My heart started to pound harder and faster, but sluggishly, taking more effort than normal to perform its task. I struggled to get my hands free and to lift them—they felt like concrete blocks at the end of wooden sticks—and it took precious seconds to relearn how to use them. There were holes in my black thermal suit and my skin looked… wrong beneath it. Burned? My heart clenched and the world wavered for a long second. I forced myself to take a deep breath of the frosty air—I could freak out properly once I was free—and raised my arms again. I clumsily slammed them into the plastic top half of the cryo-pod, hoping for a crack, a break, something, and knowing how unlikely it was.

The pods were built to withstand more than a delirious soldier. I was trapped. Trapped in a broken pod.

I pressed my lips together over a scream.

Resisted the urge to flail.

I needed to focus.

The inside of the tube was frosted over, everything on the other side, except the sparks, vague shapes and shades of grey; my eyes felt dried out and sore, along with the inside of my nose and mouth. My lips were chapped. The skin of my palms felt like paper. The ache in my arms was more pronounced now, bordering on agony.

My brain couldn't catch up, couldn't process. Everything

was ice. I shouldn't be awake. There was still cold saline circulating through my suit, still solution pumping through my blood. My body wanted to obey the chemicals and go back to sleep, but my mind wouldn't cooperate, wouldn't stop racing in circles.

Dad, March, Mom… dying over and over and over—

Paradise burning—

Ice freezing me, water drowning me, glass cutting me, fire burning me, cloth strangling me…

I was crying, gasping. Banging my hands, my head, against the tube. There was blood in my mouth, running out of my nose and from a gash on my forehead. It was hot against my cold skin. If things had been working properly, the pod would have woken me up gently, the restraint around my middle would have released, and the top of it would have been open by the time I could see.

In my sobbing and flailing, I eventually managed to hit the emergency release button on the inside of the tube. It didn't work the first time, so I hit it again, focusing intently on the round, smooth shape. And again. A strangled cry of frustration escaped my lips, a fine mist of blood splattering across the plastic.

With one more hit, warm saline solution started to run through my suit, relief from the unrelenting cold. The cryo-solution ceased and was replaced by another cocktail of chemicals, one including the combat enhancers responsible for cutting the post-cryo wake-up time down to minutes so soldiers could jump right into battle if they had to. I could feel the warmth and adrenaline sliding through my body, banishing the desire to sleep and bringing some measure of calm to my mind. The steady hum of the machinery dimmed and the pod opened slowly, jerkily, warmer air flooding over me, energizing me along with the enhancers. The darkened chamber beyond, where the rest of the soldiers still slept in their working pods, blissfully unaware that time was passing, was exposed and my vision cleared, sharpened, until every detail was visible; I'd never been on post-cryo enhancers before, and the noise, the sheer amount of information, was nearly overwhelming. The sparks flared beside me.

I'd never felt more alive.

Not for long.

Or anxious.

The sparks appeared again, reminding me of the danger, and panic, temporarily soothed, started to bubble again.

March's voice thundered through my head as he continued to taunt me. I clenched my jaw closed over a scream and fought the urge to run, since disengaging myself from the pod before it let me go wouldn't be good even if it was functioning properly. But I had to get out of that pod, get away from March, from the dreams, the memories, the dying, the—

The pod released me then, with a great shower of sparks, and I was far too aware of the needles pulling out of my skin. Remnants of the various fluids that had been pumped into me dribbled down my arms and legs as I climbed out of the pod and put my bare feet on the icy metal floor. I felt like I had been twisted, wrung out, drained, and then pumped full of something not quite right. I was too full, my skin too thin. I couldn't walk, but I had to run.

March's laughter sounded again, in my head, in the room around me. I caught sight of him in the corner of my eye, no longer a reflection but three dimensional and moving, as if he'd climbed out of the cryo-pod with me. Already on edge, the panic seized my breath and, without thought, I turned and ran towards the nearest door, away from March. A thick coil of cable came up out of nowhere and took my feet out from under me. I landed with a thud, the metal biting into the skin of my hands and feet and pressing the ports on my suit into my flesh. A few drops of blood splattered against the floor near my head.

Let go, sister. Come home to me.

It would have been so easy to lie there and give up. Without activity burning calories, the enhancer-laced solution could be harmful, maybe even fatal. It would have been so easy to give March what he wanted. But, somehow, I got to my feet. Just in time to see March skip past me and disappear through the door I'd been trying to get to.

Sluggish and unsteady, I took off after him.

Forget escaping from him. Forget running from him. I was going to catch the little bastard and be done with his ghost for good.

My bare feet slapped loudly against the metal deck, but the sound didn't echo far. I thought I heard someone call my name and ignored it in favour of chasing March. I wasn't entirely sure this version of the *Altair* was real or that any of this was happening—in the pod, everything had felt real, and I wasn't sure where the line was anymore.

Besides, I didn't want any distractions.

I had to get to March.

The corridor blurred as I entered it, shifting until I was no longer on board the *Altair*. The metal turned to wood and plaster and paint; the air became tinged with the scent of old books and spring; the portholes and the space outside them were replaced by windows looking onto green fields and blue sky. I was in the house on Earth, the one where I'd grown up, where we'd lived before taking the starward journey to Icarus, the last place where we'd been whole and happy. There'd been a swing in the big tree out back, and Lake Ontario shimmered in the distance; on clear days, we'd been able to see Toronto from our backyard, a jagged dark blue shape against the bright sky.

Hurry up, Knox! We're gonna be late!

March's voice, but joyful and pure, not twisted with hate— a snippet from some childhood memory.

Running was becoming easier, the chemicals in the solution doing their job to dull the pain and keep me moving forward, but the hall stretched endlessly in front of me and a small part of me doubted I would be able to keep up my pace for long. A cold breeze was blowing, but I paid it no mind, eager to catch up to my brother. I could hear his footsteps now, his laughter, as he ran with the confidence and exuberance of a child who had yet to take a serious tumble. I remembered the sound. The uneven slaps of his chubby feet on the hardwood of the hall; the toddler's waddle that hadn't disappeared until he was six or so.

It had been a game to him, running from me or Mom or Dad, through the halls of the old house. Bathtime, bedtime—it didn't matter. Any time he was supposed to sit still, he took off and delighted in the chase.

He laughed again, shrieking with joy until it turned harsh. Sinister. I flinched.

But I kept moving.

The floor began to shift beneath my feet, and it became harder to move as the wood softened to mud and I sunk in it up to my ankles. I stopped to pull my feet free, but even when I started running again, I was moving slower than before. As if I was trying to run against the wind.

"March! Come back!" My voice, rough from disuse, cracked over the words.

I caught sight of him for the second time, just the edge of a tiny foot as he rounded another corner. There was a sound like thunder and the world vibrated around me for a few seconds, the remembered house shaking apart. Chunks of plaster fell into the mud around me. My next step was onto a hard-packed and dusty road. The scents of spring and books were replaced by the tang of summer-dead grass and ozone; black clouds boiled above me, lightning jumping between them, waiting for the perfect moment to strike.

Another house from my past sat beside me, a house that was never a home. It was where my mom and I had moved after Icarus, when we were broken. It was squat and dingy, cramped and unwelcoming compared to the places where we'd been a family. I had never liked the place when I was younger and I didn't miss it.

I kept running, past the house, past the shiny new shuttlecar my mother had been gifted when she retired from her engineering job, and into the long grass surrounding the property. It whipped across my face, stirred by the wind and my running, and it wasn't long before I couldn't see the house anymore, couldn't hear my mother's half-hearted words telling me not to go too far in my exploration. Back then, when I'd run in the fields to escape her, I'd imagined March as he'd been in life, running beside me, his always-too-long hair snapping in the wind, his thirst for adventure infecting me. I'd tried to make it a game, tried to find some happiness.

Before the hallucination, the ghost was a near-permanent fixture in my life.

Thunder rumbled again and lightning flashed, red-tinged and wrong. The wind was picking up, growing colder, almost painfully so. The world shook and I stumbled, but when I righted myself, March was standing not too far ahead of me, in a clearing, surrounded by shadowy figures I didn't want to look too closely at.

Breathing heavily—Was the air suddenly thinner?—I sprinted across the last space between me and March and leapt, one hand extended towards the twisted, grinning face of my younger brother.

Something seized me around the waist and hauled me backwards, dragging me to the ground—the floor.

My cheek hit metal and the vision of my Earthly home broke.

I was lying on the floor of the *Altair*, in a hall that was sloping *down* into the black of space, only the faint blue shimmer of a containment barrier keeping me and Zed, the cryo-tech who had just stopped me from leaping to my death, from being sucked out of the ship. We were only a few feet away from the tear in the hull.

I rolled onto my back and stared at the burn marks on the ceiling, my chest rising and falling rapidly as my brain, my body, tried to process what had been about to happen. Beside me, Zed was nearly heaving; I didn't expect he got much exercise as rigorous as chasing me must have been.

Slowly, as the last of the vision cleared from my head, I realized an alarm klaxon was blaring and red warning lights were flashing. The ship shuddered beneath me as the containment field struggled to keep the torn shreds of the ship from breaking further apart. Thunder. Red lightning.

The *Altair* was crashing.

6.

With great difficulty, Zed managed to help me to my feet and lead me back towards the cryo-chamber. He sealed the damaged corridor off from the rest of the ship with a keypad on the wall and tucked himself under my arm as we half-ran back to where the rest of the soldiers still slept; he was taller than I was, and nowhere near as strong, but he did his best and we arrived with only more pain added to my list of current problems. I could handle more pain.

Stop resisting, Knox. Let go.

"I don't know how you're awake," Zed said once we were safely tucked away from the breach and he'd caught his breath. I propped myself against the control console in the centre of the room while Zed turned to the keyboard to start waking the room up. It was difficult to focus on him. "We're hours from the programmed wake-up time, though I suppose it's moot now, since I've gotta wake the rest of you up anyway…"

"Zed." I said his name forcefully, to both cut off his stream of consciousness and to bring his attention to me. To help me focus. "What happened to the ship?"

You should be asking what happened to you.

March kept whispering in my head, quiet and constant, but I was doing my best to ignore it, telling myself there were more important things to worry about than my delusions. More than just my life at stake. I didn't care what had happened to me, because I was alive and mostly in one piece. I would make it to Icarus and put an end to March's interference in my life.

Or not-life. It wasn't like I'd been doing much living.

Let it all go.

"The Scaleheads." Zed nearly spat the word. "A squad of them were cloaked and waiting for us. They took out the main engines, the landing gear, the starboard-side weapons, and the launch bay, so we have to take the *Altair* into atmo and hope for the best." Zed's fingers slowed momentarily and his gaze dropped, his chin sinking a little closer to his chest. His eyes were haunted; he was scared. I didn't blame him. "They caught us completely by surprise. We shot them down though, once they were visible."

"Don't we have their cloaking frequencies?"

"They've changed them. Upgraded their systems or whatever." Zed shifted his weight from foot to foot, rolled his shoulders. "We're running on minimal propulsion from the backup engines—everything's been routed to life- and cryo-support. I gotta get everyone up and warm and rigged-up before we make whatever kind of landing we're gonna make."

I assumed the other technicians who'd been there when my wave arrived—and the ones I hadn't seen—were doing the same elsewhere on the ship. If there was anyone else still alive beyond our wave. I was still bleeding, still in pain, but the enhancers were keeping it manageable for now. I didn't think they'd last much longer. Likely, the Scaleheads who had attacked us had gotten word to the rest of their soldiers stationed on and around Icarus, and they would be waiting for us. Preparing for us. Every one of the soldiers still alive on board had to be ready when we landed.

"What can I do to help?"

Zed's eyes flicked from me to the computer and back, as he realized the extent of my injuries. "Oh, shit. You don't look good. You can, uh, just wait there for right now." He typed something into the terminal on his arm, producing his stylus from somewhere as he did so. "A med team is on their way. How did you get those burns? You've been in cryo for months and there was nothing in the hall that could burn you like that."

I just shrugged.

Too busy to probe further, Zed turned back to the computer and started typing again, though he did cast a few glances my way, probably to make sure I was still standing. The sparks still fountaining from my pod stopped as he shut down the power to it for safety, and then, one-by-one, the other pods began to switch to wake-up mode. Starting with Dean's pod, the lights switched from blue to green as the warming procedure began, small jets of steam venting with a chorus of faint hissing. The medics arrived before Dean's pod opened and set to work tending my cuts and burns while I watched my fellow soldiers gather their wits about them and ignored March's voice in my head.

And his face, which kept appearing in my peripheral vision. That was new.

I tried to focus on what the medics were doing to try and drown out March's words and attempts to lure me away—I didn't want to listen to him anymore but tuning him out after so long was difficult. During the dreaming, I had realized his voice was so ingrained with my own internal thoughts that it was hard to tell where my thinking ended and his manipulation began. Was it because of him I had turned to drink in search of oblivion? Run myself into more than one injury doing laps at the gym? Was it because of him I had twisted myself towards asphyxiation in the sheets, cut my arms on glass? I didn't know. That scared me, more than anything else. Focusing on external things helped.

The medics applied a coagulation gel to the cuts on my face and made me swirl a watered-down version around my mouth to heal the cuts on my cheeks. Another gel to help with burns went on my arms before they were covered with padded black bandages that contained a numbing agent and were frequently used in field hospitals. Scaleheads utilized many fire-based weapons so our medical personnel were very adept at dealing with burns of all flavours.

You're a mess.

It's your fault, I mentally snapped, unable to tune him out any longer. *Just leave me alone.* It was a plea, one I didn't expect to work. But, tired of everything as I was, I was going to try anything.

Why do you bother, Knox? No one cares if you sacrifice your life for this.

I'm done listening to you.

"Knox?"

I started. I was leaning heavily on the control console as the medics finished their work—I was going to need either another shot of enhancers or my combat suit to be of any use when we touched down—and glaring hard at the non-reflective floor. It took me a second to realize it was Dean speaking to me, and another to realize I was glad to see him alive and whole. His eyes were bright and faintly glowing with the enhancers in his blood, and there was a restlessness to him that hadn't been there before we'd gone into cryo. Aside from not having his combat rig surrounding him, he was ready to go. He still managed to look concerned though, and I wondered briefly what I had done to deserve such kindness from him.

"You look like you got a better sleep than I did," I said without thinking.

Dean narrowed his eyes and stepped a little closer, hunching slightly so he could look at me directly. "What happened to you?"

He doesn't care.

Tears burned the back of my eyes, but I held them back. Barely. I was not an emotional person. I didn't cry in front of people, but then, I wasn't exactly at my best. "I don't even know how to answer that question," I said quietly.

The concern on Dean's face turned to outright worry. He looked around, maybe for help, but Zed was lining everyone up and sending them to suit up, and the medics were gone, so he wrapped his arm around my waist for support and we fell in line with the other soldiers. Everyone was buzzing and moving quickly, eyes glowing and muscles twitching, and I was aware of the urgency, but I didn't feel it. I felt like I was going in slow motion while everyone else was a blur around me.

Enhancer crash.

Or exhaustion.

Or both.

There is nothing for you down there, Knox. Just let go.

"Shut up," I mumbled.

"What?"

"Nothing."

Dean made a dissatisfied noise and hauled me into the storage room where our combat rigs hung, primed and waiting. Other soldiers were already in the process of attaching the metal pieces to the skin-tight under-armour suits—similar to the cryo-suits, minus all the ports except one at the base of the neck—and thankfully no one paid us much mind. It took Dean all of three seconds to find my blue-and-black armour, hanging three hooks down from his. I noticed an abundance of nicks and scratches on his armor, a couple of deep gashes from Scalehead blades on the arms, and a burn mark across the back of the helmet. Mine was not so marked up.

I changed suits slowly and somewhat awkwardly, and then started affixing the plates of my armour to it. Muscle memory made it easy for me to get geared up, and something inside settled into place with my armour; unlike almost everything else in my life, putting my rig on felt familiar in a good way. I breathed a sigh of relief when the last plate slid into place around my neck and a fresh injection of enhancers, this time blended for combat, flooded my system.

"Better?" Dean asked as he slid his helmet on. The faint glow of his eyes was visible behind his tinted visor.

"Much."

"You wanna tell me what happened?"

I put my own helmet on and found March's face waiting on the back of my visor obscuring my HUD, grin in place. And I was scared all over again. "Nope."

"All right then," he said gruffly. "Let's go kick some reptilian ass."

Yes. Let's.

7.

By the time all six hundred and twenty-five soldiers on the *Altair* were suited up and armed, the ship had reached Icarus and begun the rough drop into the planet's atmosphere; hard work for a ship never meant to go planetside. As I'd expected, Scaleheads were waiting for us to arrive. They started shooting immediately and didn't stop. The *Altair* shook and the alarms continued to blare, the hull screaming around us as it heated and the atmosphere tore at it. Thunder and red lightning. Pieces tore free from the damaged section of the ship, striking and ripping the hull as they were flung into oblivion. The alarms got louder. Angier.

March's twisted laughter through the whole ordeal was loud enough in my head to be painful and kept my heart racing. I saw flashes from the dreams with every blink—Mom and Dad;

death and burning and hate—and the cargo bay where we waited was filled with waist-high grass, soldiers dotted across the field like trees. Dean was nearby, behind me to the right, but sometimes he wasn't Dean.

Sometimes he was a Scalehead.

Sometimes all the soldiers around me were Scaleheads, the black of their armour replaced by scratched steel and leather and scales.

I'd never hallucinated like this while awake.

Never seen more than March, who was more than enough.

Not for the first time in my military career, I doubted my ability to wade into battle, to fight tooth and nail, but this time, it wasn't because I was scared of taking a life, of changing who I was in that way—it was because I was scared of what March might do or make me do. I was scared of dying, of letting go. I was scared of March getting what he wanted.

Or giving into whatever part of me March represented.

Was I crazy? Or was he really there?

I swallowed, a non-existent lump scraping against my throat. I expected the desire for a drink and its accompanying oblivion, but it didn't come. Maybe because I was steps away from Icarus and the resolution I hoped for or maybe because being eyeball-deep in battle presented its own kind of numbness. It didn't matter.

The absence of that craving sparked a small burst of hope inside.

Small, but enough to get me onto Icarus.

If I survived, maybe I could figure everything out.

If I survived, maybe I'd be okay.

The *Altair* struck the ground hard enough to knock the thoughts from my head and most of the soldiers from their feet—surviving would be no mean feat. I dropped to one knee, the other leg braced in front of me to keep my balance best I could, though I did slide a fair distance. Dean pulled a similar move nearby. The soldier on the other side of me lost their footing completely and went sliding across the textured floor, taking out two other bodies along the way. By the sound and the constant shuddering, the transport ship was skidding across the terrain, relying on friction to slow it down—whoever the pilot was deserved a medal for managing not to kill everyone in a ship never meant to touch the ground, and one with no landing gear, no engines, and missing a massive amount of hull metal besides.

I could smell burning oil and hot metal, hear air hissing and fluid dripping, feel the heat radiating from a fire somewhere. Before the ship had even come to a full stop, the hatches were opened and we began pouring out, lightning flashing around me as I joined the flood. The crush was maddening; I could taste the fear and urgency of those around me on my tongue. We were all juiced-up and armed and itching to do what we came here for.

My feet hit the ground and something inside me shifted.

Icarus.

You shouldn't have come back.

There wasn't time to do more than acknowledge that March had spoken. Scaleheads were pressing in from all sides, having tracked the ship from the moment it arrived; behind us, the *Altair* finally stopped and settled into the dirt with a loud bang. I had no idea how many Scaleheads there were, but they were all big, wide, and armed to their very pointy teeth. Powerful tails swung behind them, decimating whatever vegetation was left after our crash, and they brought with them the unrelenting stink of fuel and whatever it was they used to oil their scales and armour before battle.

The mostly flat area around me flickered between reality and the long grass of the past as I turned to face the incoming troops, surrounded on every side by blue-and-black ISC soldiers. I raised my weapon and held it close to my chest as I ran forward, just as I'd been taught.

Thunder rumbled, but the sky was blue.

I was aware of Dean to my left, unmistakable in his burned armour, and I knew he was sticking close to keep an eye on me. Five and a half months ago, I might have minded. Not so much anymore. March was still hovering in my visor. The world still flickered.

Long grass—flat plain—long grass—hallway—
Scalehead—ISC soldier—Scalehead—
I clenched my jaw. Tried to focus.

And then I was in the press of reptile and human bodies, the Scaleheads wasting no time in getting up close and personal where they were most effective. I ducked under an arching swing from the Scalehead in front of me and slammed my shoulder into its gut as I rose, hitting the hinged section of armour with all the force I could gather—in my full rig, it was enough to knock the air from the alien and send it reeling back a couple steps. I advanced on it, swinging my rifle around to launch three slugs into the meat of its body, heated plasma rounds sinking through the armour almost as if it wasn't there.

The gurgling sound it made as he died stuck in my ears.

A heavy fist connected with the back of my helmet, knocking my head around. I shook the stars from my eyes and began to turn, catching the second hit in my side, the powerful blow sending the ache right down to my flesh; I wouldn't be surprised if my armour was dented. The Scalehead lifted its heavy curved blade instead of the flamethrower strapped to its back, and I began to bring my arms up to block it.

A blast to the head took out my attacker. Plasma and brain leaked onto the ground. There was blood splattered across my visor.

There was no time to see who fired that shot.

You have no time at all.

March appeared, standing in front of me, his legs phased through the dead Scalehead from the knees down. I wanted to stop and stare him down, yell at him to leave, but I couldn't.

Even so, I must have paused for some time—even a fraction of a second would register to an enhanced soldier—because Dean's voice came in from the left, only faintly distorted by the speaker in his helmet. "Knox! Come on!" His words came out close to an order, but I was already moving again, a few steps ahead of him.

I fired as I ran, wove in and out of Scalehead arms, leapt over their tails. My weapon was hot in my hands, each round of fire knocking the temperature up a few degrees and the heat sinks struggled to keep up. The ship was turning into an inferno behind us. Every sound was loud. My heartbeat was thudding in my ears. The world was shifting around me and my breathing was getting out of control, even with the combat cocktail regulating my system. I was running for the opposite side of the Scalehead force—that was what we'd been trained to do: flank them, surround them, crush them. They were tough and smart, but when they were cornered, they could turn desperate, and would cut through even their own to get free.

Surrounding them was the hard part.

A jet of fire shot across my path. I skidded to a halt, only my combat rig keeping me upright. Another burst of fire came at my head; I felt it lick across my helmet as I dodged out of the way, and even in that split second, I began to sweat. I twisted out of the way of a third shot and found myself facing a third Scalehead.

My heart was louder than March's voice, my breathing erratic. I could feel my rig switch up its cocktail to try and counter my wild emotions, but I didn't think it was working. Nothing was changing. I lifted my rifle to fire at the third Scalehead, and then the alien did a very strange thing.

It tackled me. Held me to the ground.

I could smell its slick scales and the tang of metal from its armour and weapons. Above us, more fire.

The alien holding me down shifted.

It was Dean.

I had almost shot Dean.

My eyes began to burn and I squirmed out from under him,

back onto my feet. The battle raged on around us, the flame-welding Scaleheads already occupied with other targets, but it was all secondary. I was gulping down filtered air; I could hear my breaths wheezing out of the speaker in my helmet. My vision was going again. My rig wasn't doing its job.

March grinned at me from my visor, the readings on my HUD flickering in response.

Let go, Knox. If you just let go, it will be so much easier.

I stumbled, my feet twisting in grass that wasn't there, and dropped to the ground, scrambling backwards, my armour dinging as I hit rocks I couldn't see. There was blood all over my visor and I didn't know how it got there. I disconnected my helmet, tossed it aside, and the air was cold on my wet cheeks. I couldn't stay there, fighting Scaleheads when I couldn't be sure if they were actually aliens or not. I didn't want to be responsible for the death of an ISC soldier. I didn't want to die while I was struggling just to see.

I sobbed and realized I was crying.

I'd never been so scared.

A Scalehead launched itself towards me through the grass, its blade swinging. In a desperate move, I brought my rifle up to block the attack, but didn't try and shoot it or counter in case it wasn't really an enemy. The tip of a sword appeared through its chest, inches from my helmet—I think I screamed—and it fell on top of me. I managed to knock its sword away and avoid the tip of the killing blade.

On my hands and knees, I crawled away, scrambling to my feet after a few seconds so I could run.

"Knox!"

KNOX.

I was sobbing, gasping, tripping, dying, my tiny spark of hope extinguished. The long grass twisted in the wind on either side of me, thunder rumbled all around, red lightning flashed, and I knew I would never be free of this torment. Whether it was because of my shattered mind, because of March's ghost manipulating me, or some combination of the two, I would never be free. I was done. My hope was extinguished.

Let go, Knox. Just let go.

March's words became a meaningless rhythm, one I matched my pace to as I bolted across the open field, the end of my braid whipping me around the ears and neck as the wind pulled at it. I wasn't thinking about the deep chasms I could fall into, or the dangerous creatures I could run into—I wasn't thinking about any of the warnings we'd received when we first moved to Icarus, so long ago. I was just thinking about running, about finding some oblivion to take it all away.

I was looking for a place to finally give in to March.

It's about time.

Something seized in my chest and I dropped to my knees, my heavy armour digging small craters as it hit the ground. I doubled over, and sucked in my first deep, good breath in far too long as whatever was blocking my airway released. That's when I knew I'd found the place March wanted me to die.

When I lifted my head, I almost laughed, because of course it would be here.

At our house, in Paradise.

8.

It couldn't be anywhere else, sister.

Able to breathe properly again, my tears slowed, and I felt in control once more. Or, as in control as I had ever felt. I rose to my feet and moved towards the yard, having to actively force every step because it felt wrong to enter that place after so many years, when there hadn't been a soul there since that day; all colonization efforts in Paradise had been kept to the side of the settlement untouched in the Scalehead attack, and to the new growth, hidden behind a large wall I could see now that my visions weren't obscuring the truth.

The vegetation burned away in the Scalehead attack had grown back, though it seemed patchy and rough, and the soot and ash had been washed off the prefab structure, though no one had bothered to remove what was left of the house. Or any other of the damaged buildings nearby. They stood like broken bones jutting out of the earth, macabre gravestones for those who had died here, for the dream that had died here. The tree I had read under was dead and black, the branches on one side completely gone and the rest weathered to sharp points. The grass crackled under my armoured feet as I crossed the front yard and stood in front of what was left of the door to what should have been my home. The air smelled dusty and hot.

"This place isn't so bad, sweets. It's a lovely day, and look—there are lots of other kids around."

Dad's voice. It hurt to hear it, but I was more confused than anything. His words sounded so real that I turned in place, expecting to see him on the path, standing in front of the shuttlecar carrying our belongings. But there was no one there. I was alone. Even March remained quiet. He may have wanted me to come here, but he didn't like being there anymore than I did.

"I don't like it here."

"Knox, you've got to give it a chance, okay? We just got here."

"Why did we have to leave home?"

Dad kneels down in front of me and tucks some of my hair behind my ear before cupping my cheek with the same hand. "You know why, sweets. We came here for Mom's work, and to explore a new planet. We're the farthest human colony from Earth. Isn't that cool?"

I sigh, roll my eyes. "I guess."

"You love space, don't you? You've been reading novels about exploring the stars and new planets pretty much since you were old enough to read. You're telling me you're not excited to be here?"

I want to tell him that I'm not, but I'd be lying. He's right—I have dreamed about doing something like this hundreds of times, but for some reason it never occurred to me that I'd have to leave Earth, leave everything I knew, everything safe, to do it. I sigh and look at Dad, who is waiting patiently for my answer.

"I'm scared," I say.

"I know, sweets. So am I. This place is beautiful, but dangerous. But as long as we're careful, and we listen to the soldiers who are here to protect us, we'll be fine. We can help make this place a real paradise for humanity."

I can't stop myself from chuckling. Not because I think he's joking or because I think what he said is amusing, but because the sentiment is so hopeful, so bright, it just makes me happier about the whole thing.

He smiles and leans in to kiss my forehead. "That's my girl. Now, grab a box and let's start unloading. Mom and March will be along in a minute."

I take the small crate Dad hands me and smile up at him before heading into the house.

I had forgotten that moment, one like so many others in my life before Dad was killed. But now it was precious and I found myself smiling as I gazed at the overgrown stone of the pathway.

When was the last time I'd smiled like that?

When was the last time I'd had a *good* memory?

But what is that worth when you're still alone?

But I wasn't alone, was I? I'd come back to Icarus with hundreds of other soldiers, and though I didn't know most of them, I did know Dean. Dean, who had stuck close the moment he realized something was going screwy in my head. And I knew

Zed, who had promised to keep me alive and had delivered, despite what had gone wrong with my cryogenic sleep.

Maybe I could find someone to get to know as a real friend. Maybe Dean would become a real friend.

Maybe I *could* tell him everything and wouldn't think I was mad.

"I know you're scared, hon, but the technology is safe. I promise."

I don't want to believe Mom, or feel soothed by her words, but I am. A little. "What if I don't wake up?"

"You will."

"But—"

"Knox." She says my name like she's mad, but she's probably just annoyed. I know she wants to go check on March and Dad, and I know she wants to talk to the techs before she goes under, and my freak out is eating into her time to go through her checklist. "It is scary. I'm a little scared too," she says quietly. Like it's a secret. "But when we wake up, we'll be in our new home. Paradise."

She smiles at me and I smile back, calmed for the moment. I don't let myself think about what I'm about to do as I nod. "Okay."

"Okay." She tucks some hair behind my ear and then nods to the man in the white coat standing nearby. "See you soon."

I climb into the pod as instructed and watch Mom until she's gone. Somewhere nearby, March laughs.

That was probably the last conversation Mom and I had before Dad and March died and our lives changed so completely. As soon as we'd arrived on Icarus, she'd become so busy we rarely saw her, and never for more than maybe an hour at a time.

She'd been working to make Paradise a home for us and for anyone else who came there. Making homes among the stars had been her lifelong dream.

March was growing angrier with me; I could hear the venom in his voice as he whispered and hissed in my head, tried to make me walk into the house, to make me lie down and give up. Grass whispered against the armour plates on my legs and thunder grumbled all around me, but though I knew it wasn't real, I was afraid of what it meant.

Death.

I could still feel my death in every dream.

I turned and looked back at the house, expecting to see March's semi-transparent form there, watching, waiting. Smiling.

"Did you see our rooms?" March yells as he comes flying out the front door. He's grinning from ear to ear, his hair messy, wild.

Mom clucks her tongue as she walks by and tries with one hand to tame his mop. "Your hair grows like weeds, March. We'll have to cut it again soon."

He bats her hands away and starts running towards me again. "Did you see them, Knox?"

I pull my gaze away from the forest in the distance and smile down at my brother. He's been yelling and running non-stop since we arrived, eager to see, touch, and try everything he can get his hands on. Even taste in a few cases; according to him, the walls taste like hand sanitizer. I don't want to know how he knows what hand sanitizer tastes like.

"Yeah, I saw them." My room is about half the size of the one I left on Earth, and it's right beside March's instead of at the opposite end of the

hall. "They're neat."

"This whole place is neat!" March's voice squeaks over his excitement and I can't help but laugh. Sometimes, my little brother is cute.

His grin widens when he sees me smiling, and he throws his arms around my waist, hugging me tightly. I try to tamp down the affection I feel for him—he's my little brother—*but I return the hug and then rub my knuckles against his scalp before running away across the grass.*

He gives a wild yelp and follows me, enthralled by the game of tag.

Another pleasing moment, forgotten. Buried by the weight of my guilt and the horror of reliving the worst day of my life again and again and again. I had forgotten how March and I had leaned on each other in those few days on Icarus, how my younger brother had shown uncharacteristic strength and compassion, how he'd known I needed to laugh more than ever after being taken away from Earth. He'd been more excited than sad about our new adventure and wanted me to feel the same. He'd made it his goal to make me smile like he did.

There were tears on my cheeks again, and they were bittersweet.

What else had I forgotten or buried? What else had I missed out on, living surrounded by the darkness in my life as I had been?

By letting March control everything?

I wanted more moments like the ones I was being reminded of. I wanted new memories I wouldn't smother.

NO.

That spark of hope I felt before our crash landing came back, stronger, brighter. March didn't like those memories, those thoughts, but I didn't care. I clung to the hope burning inside, to my new desires, and I turned to start heading back to the battlefield, back to the *Altair*. I didn't know where my helmet had ended up, but my rifle was still strapped to my back, and my armour seemed to be functioning again. I wasn't in any shape to continue fighting—I didn't want to put anyone else in danger—but I could help the techs and crew of the ship. If nothing else, I could protect them.

I was done hiding.

That statement turned out to be truer than I meant it.

A Scalehead, wounded and wild eyed, with the remains of a flamethrower on their back, was approaching, no doubt drawn by the sight of a lone soldier. There was blood and drool dripping from their jaws. Most of their armour was gone, but the reek of desperation clung to them, and that more than anything else unnerved me. I pulled my rifle around, took aim, and fired, but the weapon must have taken some damage somewhere along the way because all three shots missed and it heated up far faster than it should have.

March giggled.

The Scalehead saw their moment and took it, lunging for me with their clawed hands stretched out in front. They tore the gun from my hands, from its connection to my armour, and tossed it aside faster than I could react; something was wrong with my suit after all because I could feel the enhancer crash taking over me again. I blocked the Scalehead as they grabbed for my head, the only unprotected part of me, but I couldn't stop their other hand.

Claws dug trenches in my skull as they took hold of my hair and threw me into the wall of the house. My armour absorbed most of the shock, but my bones were still rattled, and I slumped to the ground in a heap. Even dazed as I was, I could see the cracks in the wall, tempered and made brittle by the heat of the attack and the weather of intervening years.

I rolled to my feet as the Scalehead came for me again, stepping to the side and using their own momentum and my hand on their back to drive them into the wall. There was a loud crack as the wall gave in, followed by the sound of shattering plastic, and my attacker was left drawing themselves out of the rubble, new wounds leaving streaks of blood on the pale material as they moved. They clawed at the broken tank on their back until it came free, and tossed the remains of their weapon into the remains of my house.

I scrambled for my rifle, managed to get to it, and get a few more shots off as the Scalehead shook off the impact. One hit their shoulder and they bellowed, but the other two hit the house behind them, one finding its way to the fuel tank, which ignited in a foul-smelling burst.

I tried to shoot again, but the rifle overheated and, even through my armour, it was too hot. I tossed it aside, and then the Scalehead was there.

Their tail swung out and caught me around the knees, knocking me to the ground. I only just kept my head from slamming off the ground. I got my feet up in time to halt the Scalehead's advance, bending my knees and then thrusting my legs out to send the alien back a few steps; the machinery of my rig whined angrily as it reset. The rigs made us stronger, faster, and more durable, but, just as the cryo-pods, they weren't infallible.

And mine seemed to also be vulnerable to March's whims.

Or was I imagining that?

I felt the rig fail the moment the Scalehead grabbed my ankle, knocking me off balance, and dragging me across the ground. It became deadweight around me, a metal prison. The flow of the enhancer cocktail into my body stopped and I let out a frustrated yell at March, who had appeared, standing above my head, hands on his hips.

Just let go. It'll be so much easier than this.

I snarled up at him. He wouldn't take any more from me.

I let out a primal yell and threw my arms above my head, right through my brother, to grab at the ground and try to use it, and the weight of my gauntlets, to slow me down. The Scalehead growled when I began to struggle and stopped moving before they turned to adjust their grip on my leg. Letting my anger and fear fuel me, I kicked my leg free of the Scalehead's hands and tried to move away.

"Stop this," I ground out, directing the words at March as much as the reptile in front of me. They cocked their head, like they didn't understand; maybe their translator was broken or maybe mine was. "Stop."

Confused, the Scalehead stilled, watching me with their red-gold eyes, blood and drool sliding through the spaces where teeth used to be. They were breathing heavily.

My suit flickered to partial life around me.

The Scalehead saw it light up. And lunged.

There was no time for me to move before they grabbed me again, fingers sliding between the plates of my rig and hauling me up high before slamming me down on their raised knee.

I screamed.

Guttural laughter rumbled from the Scalehead as they dropped me to the ground. I tried to roll away, but everything in me protested. Loudly. Thunder joined the laughter, and then March's laughter was there too, higher-pitched and agonizing.

March was going to get what he wanted.

The Scalehead's foot appeared on my stomach. My armour screeched as it stepped down. It kept laughing.

Let go, Knox. There's nothing left for you here. There's nothing left for you anywhere.

I screamed again, but this time it was as I grabbed the Scalehead's foot and pushed it off me. I felt things in me tearing, but I managed to lift the foot enough to roll free. It hurt so bad I almost passed out, but whatever enhancers were left in my blood gave me the boost I needed to get out and up on my feet. The metallic tang of blood reached my nose and I wasn't sure if it was mine or the wounded alien's; now that I was up, I could see their scales were slick with fresh blood and they were swaying. Thunder sounded above, and there was a flash of light.

I launched myself at the Scalehead, wrapping my arms around their middle and riding them to the ground. We skidded a few feet and when we stopped, I straddled their stomach, clamping my knees tightly to either side and making sure the metal plate over my left knee dug right into its wounded flank before my rig went dead again. They howled. Blood dripped from my nose and mouth and head, landed on their armour. My entire world was pain.

But I took their lower jaw in one hand, it's upper jaw in the other, and I wrenched them apart.

Stop fighting it, Knox. You know it's time to let go.

I didn't respond to March, just ground my teeth together and adjusted my position to get better leverage as I used whatever juice remained in my suit, and the sheer weight of the thing, to ramp up my strength and tear the Scalehead's lower jaw free from their face.

The sound they made was unlike anything I had ever heard.

The Scalehead thrashed beneath me, but I held on. Blood fountained out. I closed my mouth and eyes and reached blindly for their belt, hoping there was still a knife—or anything sharp—around. There was.

I took it and cracked one eye so I could be sure not to miss.

The blade slid through scales and the flesh beneath easily, and sliced the spinal cord like it was nothing.

My foe went still beneath me.

My vision waved and the pain overwhelmed me. I fell to the side, landed on my back.

That's it. Let go.

I thought I could feel a hand stroking my hair back from my face. Wind blew across my skin and my sight went in and out. Beside me, what was left of my home in Paradise burned steadily, whatever fuel the Scaleheads used more than a match for the old prefab constructions of Earth. Thunder rumbled again, and I realized it wasn't a vision. A storm had blown in and dark clouds were spreading quickly over the crystalline blue above, the first few drops of rain heralding what was coming.

A slow smile spread across my face as lightning flashed above—purple-white, not red. I'd never seen it rain on Icarus before.

Knox, just let go.

"Knox!"

My eyelids were heavy, so I closed them. I felt the rain on my face, washing the blood and sweat away. It mingled with tears I hadn't realized I was crying, and then I slipped into the darkness, listening to the approaching footsteps and knowing, *trusting*, that Dean wouldn't let me die.

I just needed to sleep for a while.

9.

"Hold on, Knox."

I could hear Dean, his deep voice cutting through the fog of pain and confusion and—Was that fear?—and I focused on him, even though I couldn't open my eyes to see him. I didn't want to slip into sleep or unconsciousness again. I didn't want to go where March could get me, but it was getting more and more difficult to resist the pull of oblivion—even halfway delirious as I was, it wasn't lost on me that the thing I'd spent over half my life chasing was now the thing I wanted least. I could still hear March, but his voice was faint, like it was coming from a long way away, or like he was weak, losing his hold on this world, on me, on whatever was keeping him here.

Maybe the Scalehead had knocked some clarity into me by throwing me around.

My suit sputtered and died again, and my pain, no longer being dulled by the last of the cocktail being pumped through my suit, started to escalate.

I groaned and March growled.

I told you I wouldn't be that easy to get rid of.

I heard *that* loud and clear, but I also heard the increased strain in his voice. There was no spare brain power to enjoy whatever small victory that represented though, since I was in agony, my pain ramping up with every beat of my heart. I could hear myself screaming, but I felt removed from it, detached, unwilling to face the fact that I was imprisoned in my own armour, my own body. I was floating above myself, lost in a sea of tall grass and wooden hallways and memories I'd lost.

"There's a med team on the way, Knox. Just hold on."

Let go.

I kept screaming.

"Soldier!" Dean barked, resorting to what he knew; I wondered if Dean had been an officer when he wasn't a member of the reserves. "Listen to my voice!"

I wanted to scream again, but managed to keep it in, to listen to Dean's command, and push off March's influence. My sight was blurry when I cracked one eyelid, and the rain didn't help, but Dean was close and easy to focus on, kneeling on one knee directly to my left. He had one hand on his rifle, ready to leap into action if another Scalehead showed up, and the other hand at my neck, checking for a pulse or measuring my heart rate. I couldn't feel his fingers on my skin. I couldn't feel anything beyond the pain. I knew things in my body were broken, but I didn't know if that was why I couldn't move, or if the weight of my suit was keeping me pinned.

March was growing clearer again, his grin possessive, almost demonic as I marinated in the agony.

Another scream bubbled up in my throat and I wanted to thrash and flail with the sound. I opened both my eyes, sobbed with the relief of even those small movements, and tried to anchor myself back in my body. I thought about how the soft rain on my face should feel, how the scent and sound of the smouldering prefab house nearby should smell and sound—I focused as hard as I could on Dean's touch, on the only human connection I had until I found feel the pressure of his fingers, the roughness of his skin.

"Dean," I managed to say, his name coming out small and trembling. I wanted to say something else, to ask him if he thought I was dying, but my throat stopped working and all that came out were strangled noises.

I won't go without you.

Dean moved closer to my head, keeping a hand on me. I kept my eyes glued to him even though he kept going out of focus; I was crying again. Or still crying. I had no idea how much time had passed since my battle with the Scalehead, but I didn't think it had been that long. Dean had been on his way when I'd fallen, right? He would have called the medics immediately.

"You're going to be all right, Knox. Just hang on. I can see the shuttle now."

That was good.

I just had to hang on.

Dean wouldn't let me die.

I wasn't alone.

Let go.

But it would hurt so much less to give in, wouldn't it?

"Hey, Knox, look at me." There was a note of panic in Dean's voice, like he could feel me slipping. "Keep your eyes on me." An order again.

My head had rolled to one side as far as it could in my rig, but I didn't remember deciding to look that way. I could see the medical shuttle now too, a white blip on the horizon, still some distance out. Just a few more minutes maybe. Dean put a hand on either side of my head and gently turned it so I was looking up at him again, up at the sky, though he kept his head and shoulders over me to keep the rain from falling on my face.

"I don't want to move you too much so I'm just going to hold your head."

I wanted to respond, nod, something, but instead, I just stared at him as tears continued to run from my eyes and my body continued to hurt.

"I know you're scared. The medics are almost here. They'll get you stabilized and then take you to the field hospital in Paradise. I've seen soldiers nowhere near as stubborn as you come back from worse. You'll recover fine. Then you can tell me what the hell happened to you, okay?"

It was phrased as a question, but something told me filling him in wasn't going to be up for debate once I was capable of speech again.

If.

March shimmered into view beside Dean. I wanted Dean to start, to react to March's presence, but March wasn't real. He couldn't actually be standing here. There was nothing for Dean to react to. March kept his eyes on me. That glare was a weight on my chest, one that made me cough, spitting blood onto my face and armour and Dean's helmet. March laughed. Reached out and touched me, his fingers sliding into my flesh.

I went cold, the feeling familiar from my cryogenic torment, and sobbed again. Dean looked around and, satisfied we weren't in any immediate danger, removed his helmet quickly, so he could get his hand back on my cheek, supporting my head. His eyes were still glowing a bit, his suit free to do its job, but he smiled and the inhuman edge the enhancers gave his face vanished.

"You're tough. You can hang on."

I felt one corner of my mouth twitch. Dean snorted softly, a laugh.

The sound of the medical shuttle reached my ears, a low hum. Still not there, but closer.

They won't make it in time.

They would.

They had to.

I wanted them to.

Above me, Dean morphed into a Scalehead, mouth open and dripping, razor teeth inches from my face. The hum of the shuttle turned into the whisper of grass, the storm above amplified until the thunder rattled my bones and the lightning buzzed along my skin. March cackled, keeping his fingers embedded in my body, my soul, a reminder of what he had done, the power he had. The power I had given him. The tears flowed faster from my eyes and, even though I had watched Dean become the alien, the fear inside grew until I was shaking uncontrollably, the movement making me hurt worse. The Scalehead growled and grunted, their hands pressing against my cheeks until I thought my head was going to burst.

I couldn't stop the next scream that built in my chest, my battered body arching against its metal prison, and things inside me never meant to move shifted.

The pain stopped.

But I knew that wasn't a good thing.

You are mine, sister. Mine.

I wouldn't let him take me, wouldn't give in. He had been hovering around for years, twisting my guilt and sadness into something black and angry, manipulating my desire for solitude, for freedom from him into a thirst for oblivion. He had taken every one of my darkest thoughts and feelings and amplified them until they were all-consuming. He'd taken every chance I had to move on away until it was just March and me and the memories, until all he had to do was show up and I was too terrified to fight, until I almost craved the glimpse into the life that had been. I had moved through life numb and uncaring and alone, not because my family had died due to my actions, but because March's ghost had kept me isolated and afraid to get close to anyone else.

No more.

It didn't matter if letting go would be painless and easy.

Painless and easy were not what I wanted. Not anymore.

I forced my eyes to meet March's in the middle of the maelstrom he was whipping the world into. Forced my lips to move, my voice to work.

"You—are—dead."

Because you let me go.

"Because you ran. Go. Run again. Be with Mom and Dad. Leave me alone."

You are—

I willed him gone. With everything I had left, I pushed against his presence in my head, an inky black splotch bleeding through the fabric of me, until something snapped.

March vanished.

My vision went dark.

And I died.

10.

For the first time in fifteen years, I slept and didn't dream.

I woke up tucked into a rigid bed, and in a half-reclined position, the sheets holding me in place and keeping the chill off. There were several pillows propped behind me and I was very stiff. For long moments, I couldn't figure out where I was, but details slowly started to resolve around me: wires connecting me to a small forest of machines around my bed, all softly beeping and displaying information; low light bouncing off a thin white curtain; low voices nearby, but not close enough to understand; a sterile smell that wanted to bring bad memories to the surface but didn't quite manage it because that smell meant I was safe.

I was in a hospital.

I was alive.

And, also for the first time in fifteen years, I was alone in my head—the only voice I could hear my own, and that shroud of self-hate and despair was mostly gone. I didn't want anything except some water. And maybe to go back to sleep.

March was gone.

I sobbed, and the sound burst from me without issue, without pain. The tears that followed were happy, relieved. I started to laugh.

There would be work to do with my mental state, but March was gone.

A flurry of movement outside the curtain heralded the arrival of two big men: one was in a white coat with a stethoscope around his neck and the look of a former soldier about him, and the other was Dean, decked out in his uniform and looking much less Scaleheady than he had the last time I remembered seeing him.

"Hey, soldier," he said.

"Is everything all right, PFC Abernathy?" The doctor stepped up to the side of my bed and began a standard examination, manually checking my vitals and comparing them to the readouts around him, looking for any signs of distress. His brow was furrowed and the corners of his mouth were drawn down. He was a serious man. "Any pain?"

I considered how I felt. I'd been out long enough for my body to feel strange and unfamiliar. Or maybe it just felt strange to be fully anchored to it again after so long living a half-life. "No. No pain," I said after a few seconds. "Well, yes, a little, but I'm assuming that's normal." I looked up at the doctor. His lined face had relaxed. It was a kind face. I felt safe in his care. "But I'm fine. Need some water though." My voice cracked over the words, proving my point.

He narrowed his eyes but handed me a cup of water he'd poured from the jug on a table next to my bed and continued his checks. Behind him, Dean laughed. It was a good sound. After a few minutes, several more questions about how moving felt and about my injury sites, and a reminder to drink the water slowly, the doctor left, giving Dean and I an odd look before he disappeared behind the curtain.

"How long have I been out?" I asked, knowing the information would be more palatable coming from Dean.

"Almost three weeks."

"Holy shit." But I was smiling. Three weeks with no dreams and no near deaths—or no near deaths other than the one that had brought me to the hospital. No wonder I felt so good. "How bad was I hurt?"

Dean leaned on the bed near my knees and crossed his arms over his chest. "Bad. I wasn't sure you were alive when they loaded you into the medical shuttle. You were pale and barely moving, and you'd closed your eyes." Dean cleared his throat and ran a hand back over his hair. "At the field hospital, Dr. Costa—he just left—did the initial examination, stabilized you, and then sent you here, to Eden."

I frowned. Eden was another colony on Icarus, the first one to be established on the planet and the biggest. A bloody battle with the Scaleheads took place shortly after it had been built, but since then, the settlement had been fortified and had grown exponentially. I hadn't known there was a hospital in Eden, and there was something strange about still being on Icarus, but half a planet away from where I'd nearly died, from where I'd lost my family.

After taking another sip of water, I asked, "Did they tell you what my injuries were?"

"Yeah. Are you sure you want to know?" I nodded and Dean gave one of his one-armed shrugs. "Your spine was broken, along with several ribs, and most of your body was bruised pretty heavily. Your burns hadn't healed at all, and your heart stopped twice before they declared you stable. And that's just what the doctors told me."

I pressed my lips together. "Surprised I survived."

"Me too, as much as I kept telling you to hang on."

A weak smile crossed my lips. "Anything else?"

"They kept you in a coma for most of the rebuilding process, but even after all your bones were whole again, and they were sure you would be able to walk, it was like you didn't want to wake up."

I was positive I hadn't wanted to wake up. Twelve years without a dreamless sleep. Twelve years of torture and confusion and darkness. "Did they ever think I *wasn't* going to wake up?"

"Not that they told me. The nurses kept up their routine—apparently they talked to you quite a bit—and were sure you would wake up in your own time."

"Weird."

Dean rolled his eyes. I knew he wanted to ask me again what had happened, but he was giving me time. I appreciated that. "Yeah. The doc also said you'll have some physical therapy ahead, but your surgeries went as well as they could have, and you should feel stronger soon."

"I feel great."

He snorted. "You look like hell."

"Thanks." I shared a laugh with Dean, and then asked, "Why did you come looking for me on Icarus? And why did you stay?" I wasn't really sure I wanted the answers, but it had been a long time since anyone gave a damn about me or gone out of their way to help me. It had been even longer since I'd done the same for someone else.

Dean sighed and scrubbed a hand over his face. Maybe he'd been dreading the question. "You needed help. I knew it almost from the moment I met you—anyone who bothered to look would have seen it. And I knew you weren't going to ask for it." He sighed, and fell silent for a few seconds, but I didn't doubt he would continue speaking when he was ready. His eyes were far away and I'd seen the expression enough times in the mirror to know he was remembering something. Someone. "I've seen people fade away before, because they didn't want to or didn't know how to ask for help—people I loved. I don't know you well, Knox, but I recognized the signs, and I wasn't about to stand by and let you go without at least trying to help."

My eyes suddenly burned with more tears, and though I didn't fight them off, they didn't fall. Just bubbled in the corners and blurred my vision. The waves of emotion passing through me felt good. Clean, even.

It would have been so easy for Dean to stay silent that day

on the ISC base, so easy to strike up a conversation with someone else. He could have kept walking and let the sullen soldier keep to herself. But he had started a conversation with me, and he had listened to everything I wasn't saying.

I sniffed and lifted my chin a bit. "What are you, some kind of fucking saint?"

Dean snorted another laugh and then moved closer so he could put a hand on my shoulder. Following an impulse I hadn't felt in ages, I grabbed him and pulled him close enough for a hug. My battered body protested quietly, but I barely noticed; it felt wonderful to move, and even better not to be afraid of what might happen when I did. After a second of surprised stillness, Dean hooked an arm around my shoulders and gently returned the gesture. He was warm and solid and real.

"Thank you," I said softly.

My chest felt like it was going to burst, but I let the feeling flood through me instead of fighting it. Dean stepped back but squeezed my shoulder before he let go and gave me a small smile. He may have been a fairly open person, but I wasn't sure he was comfortable with displays of emotion.

In the ensuing silence, I tensed, waiting for March's voice, his face, to appear, for him to mock or taunt or berate as he'd done a thousand, a million, times before. But even though there were any number of reflective surfaces within sight, there was not one sign of my brother's ghost. The blackness I had associated with him was nearly gone from my thoughts, and I took my next breath unafraid.

Finally, I had my solitude.

www.ingramcontent.com/pod-product-compliance
Lightning Source LLC
Chambersburg PA
CBHW061244140726
47998CB00006B/2081